MAMA CHAVA TELLS THE TRUTH

Tales Of Trauma, Transformation & Transcendence

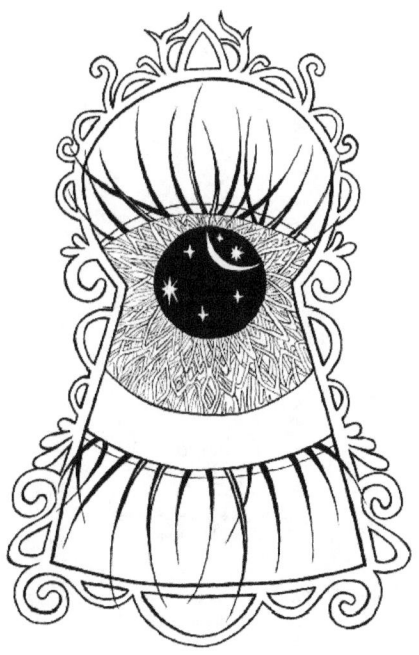

Written with love by
EVE McDAVID

AUTHOR
Eve McDavid

EDITOR & PROOFREADER
Eve McDavid

COVER DESIGN AND TYPESETTING
Sandra Jiménez

ORIGINAL ARTWORK
Melissa Rose

ISBN
979-8-9924319-0-2

To Matt, who led us here.
And for Ruby Ann and Arthur Claude,
our Brave Little Bandits.

OUR JOURNEY

A Welcome from Mama Chava

Welcome, welcome, come on in,
welcome to my home.

It's a place of peace, not grief,
you'll feel it in your bones.

Here we'll sit and take a beat,
I'll wrap you cozy-comfy,
your work is done, let's have some fun,
just wait for what's in store.

Help me tell the stories that we know,
we've heard them all before.
But this time listen up, my dear,
as we open up this door:

to fresh old tales of truth and hurt,
of love and terror, too,
because we all, from the time we're small,
must adapt in order to get through.

Oh yes, there's hope! Because of you,
you chose to take this path,
to keep a mind so curious,
new beauty rising from the ash.

So tuck right in and listen closely
to the beats within your heart.
It's time for feeling, it's time for healing,
it's time for us to start.

WHISTLEBLOWER

A CHIME,
A WHISTLE
A TRAIN THROUGH YOUR VEINS,
HOWEVER YOU'RE CALLED

PAY ATTENTION.

IT'S HAPPENING NOW
TO SEND YOU A TRUTH.

OPEN YOUR MIND, HEART AND SOUL,

LEARN THE LESSON.

You are a guest of nature, behave.

Friedensreich Hundertwasser

Her Beginning

The pain in her neck comes from Boston.
The feeling of living accosted.
Run down and mistreated, depleted, exhausted,
from the fight of her life
for her spirit held hostage.

By 33, that life expired,
a family curse took hold inside her.
Her weeping womb became her tomb.
But then! Four lives 'anew burst free.

The Strongest Girl in the World

There was once a brave little girl.
She had the strength to heal the whole world.
She could feel it inside, her love made her thrive,
and she only used it for good.
And the brave little girl was so strong.
So damn strong she felt it like a song.
She was powered by love, a bright light from above,
fit to her specs, like a hand in a glove.
Love was her body's own rhythm,
that her energy built for its system.
A train through her veins, she felt its refrain,
when it set her alarm to assess.
She knew every tense meant *"put up your defense!"*
When she felt its chim-chime, she listened.

The chime was how the girl felt,
like seeing the right in the good and the help.
Hearing good words of praise, she felt so ablaze;
she knew good from bad, feeling softness not sad,
her best defense was her own powerful senses,
like smelling the sweet in sugary treats,
not leaving bad tastes with words that lay waste.
Though her choices the same,
"choose joy or choose pain,"
she started to play by her rules.

And play as she did, born a secret detective,
dropped into her mission, though never elective.
So cunning, she selected the feelings she elected
to feel when she knew she'd feel best.
Like all little girls, she still suffered pain,
but pain can have purpose, it's never in vain.
Her pain had a name, of blame and deep shame,
the feeling she felt when it's wrong,
that feeling of fear in a mean face or a sneer,
and sharpened the words to her song.
But, when push came to shove, she always chose love,
and led by example with kindness and poise,
rising above with her head held up high,
she never fell prey to the noise.

Her system was built with a plan of the plan,
a failsafe back-up in case of **The Man.**
From there she learned the meaning of hurt:
"Know that you're strong and get on alert!"

For that brave little girl, her home was quite tricky,
parental demands were craven and sickly.
So the brave little girl looked to ring her good ring,
her chime when she needed to feel some good things.
And fought hard for herself to protect,
shouting "there's no place for your foot on my neck!"
Step-by-step she would learn, it was always her turn
when she stood up for herself in the fight.
So she set little traps and she kicked tiny tires,
testing her powers on all kinds of fires.
She tried all the limits, she pushed through the bounds,
but she found herself crashing and coming unwound.

When she was safe, she could turn down the dial,
finding grownups who loved her, greeted with smiles.
They knew she was brave and they knew she was smart,
they'd never imagine she hurt from the start.
She did well in school, a teacher's delight!
They loved her, and she them, she was so very bright.
The more she learned and loved and cared,
her chime was alive, she didn't have to be scared.
And they helped, the people who knew how to help,
those she asked when she knew how she felt.
She found doctors, professors, professionals galore -
"Keep adults in the room who keep the right score!"

But the brave little girl who lived so many lives,
still lived at home with one secret to hide.
Her home was not safe, never been, never was,
'cause change isn't an agent born without love.
Why? she would ask, but her game was the same,
She could look to our history to see all the blame.
All the men who were mean and so little and small
who chose to hurt children, the most precious of all.
And the women who hurt because men hurt them too,
but scared for too long, they can no longer do.

So those men become dads and those dads do their thing,
they hurt folks at work or in bars or a ring.
But some of those dads do the hurt right at home,
where their brave little children have nowhere to roam.

And the moms make a start, they try to stand up,
But sometimes they wither and fail to show up.
Some moms try to leave, make a place that is safe,

but then life finds a way in the way of that place.
And these rudderless parents tangle inside themselves,
Hurting little ones meant for safety, above nothing else.

But this was all wrong, her chime would then crumble,
How could those parents make those cruel rumbles?
OF yelling of fighting of hitting of hands,
OF counting the chits of those from our lands,
OF feelings of hurt and fear for her health,
OF words that would stick, no matter her stealth.
OF barbs that smell mean and taste even worse,
a strange desperation now consumed hurt.
If she stayed in that home, she'd never be safe,
And that brave little girl got tired of her face.
She'd been waiting for chimes she knew wouldn't ring,
when the bad feels that bad, it means only one thing.

Who could she trust? She kept getting it wrong.
Alliances scrambled, animals too far gone.
She was scared, more than ever, but she was still brave,
she'd fought how she could with her love to save.

So that brave little girl, conditioned for good
lived out her days with an invisible hood.
She played down her pain, amassed more good gains,
hiding her holocaust laced up with shame.

Still, that brave little girl worked hard all the time,
finding her strength and rhythm and rhyme.
She spoke up and spoke out to the people who knew,
'cause people need help when they need to get through.
That brave little girl fought her way out of her house,
the courage of a lion in her size of a mouse.

It never was perfect, all that hurt left to heal
though she kept up her march, her display of appeal.
She kept it quiet, *"it's over, it's done,"*
but the show never stopped when the girl tried to run.
So she turned up her talents, her skills of disguise,
she worked for her things, a life as a spy.
She was brilliant and bold, more wily than most,
meanwhile her chime fell prey to a host.
"That's old news", she thought, *"it's gone with the trash,"*
But pangs of old pain then deepend the gash.

For one day was different, her best no longer the same.
On that day she faced the hurt and the shame.
Her chimes were still on, though murky and frayed,
She could no longer hear it when people came to say
all the good things they knew about the brave little girl,
whose powers they hoped could now heal the world.
So she sat in the shame and gave way to the pain,
because after so long what's the use?
When she looked in the mirror it still wasn't clearer,
could it be that her chime led her wrong?
Still, she knew who she was wasn't one of those thugs,
and she named those things

CHILD

ABUSE

Next, she remembered a lesson from a bold woman she knew
"Use your voice, it's your choice,
you're ready to break through!"
With her voice came new power for the brave little girl,
She hoped there was still time to reset the world.

So she looked to the good ones, the adults in the room.
The ones there to listen, not to assume.
The ones who looked out with courage and care,
the ones who showed up with little fanfare.
They came to help, they showed her the way,
When she now looked inside, she knew what to say.

The brave little girl was ready this time,
"But first, tell me why, how'd I miss those red lines?"

And the chime rang aloud, this time with spirit!
It was so very important for the brave girl to hear it.

> **"Search for the right and the good and the true,**
> **these parts are alive, they feel just like you.**
>
> **The parts that hear and hurt and can see,**
> **the parts that bellow 'stay away from me!'**
>
> **The parts that trust when the feeling feels bad,**
> **and see through the noise when they're made to feel sad.**
>
> **The parts that live and can breathe and can jump,**
> **the parts that reveal if there's ever a lump.**

The parts that are quiet but awake in a flash,
the parts that stay calm in case of a crash.
These are your parts! They showed you the way,
teaching new lessons to save you each day!"

The brave little girl got up from the floor,
she rooted out the shame and lept for the door.
For in her real world were still people and parts
that came in the form of scars on her heart.
But she practiced and tried and each time she was brave,
no longer so little fighting wolves in a cave.
She chose her choice, shared her voice and her heart
and decided

"right here, right now, I know I can start –
to remember my parts that are good and are true,
and those no longer needed for me to 'get through'."

I'll put my foot down, I'll ask for respect,
of course I know beauty's not found in a threat!"

A strong woman became of that brave girl she was,
strengthening the hearts of those whom she loves.

She seeks the hurt and the fear and the pain,
and sends in her system to pierce its refrain.

She hits the high notes to hear songs of her own,
ones without price so she'll never disown.

She studies the subjects with important signals,
like be who YOU are despite all the jingles.

She reads honest books about determination and faith,
and ones with the truth about hardship and race.

She hears the right words with affirmation and pride,
not ones laced with rot unleashed and alive.

She eats the good foods because they're rich and they're safe,
knowing right from wrong without ever a taste.

Now a brave woman, she lives with her powers,
She is the master of all of her hours.
She finds her same people who share her kind of light,
caring first for those who gave shelter in her dark night.
She makes more good choices, she gets to say "when!"
and she knows what it means to be a good friend.
That brave little girl is the woman we know,
she is kind, she is smart and she now runs her show.
The brave woman's system now so very true,
with love and hope for the world, she knew what to do:

she shared her chime
with brave little girls just like
YOU.

Bravest Little Boy In The World

There once was a brave little boy,
who had the strength to tell his own story.
He loved with his heart, his most courageous part,
and those who felt his love became whole.

He made a life, through pain and through strife,
with the brave little girl we all know,
the one with the love, that shines through from above,
and found themselves healing in love.

That brave little boy is the man the girl needed,
he saved her life with his care,
through strength and through grace,
he found her this place,
so they could finally build new dreams.

The brave little boy still hurts, though now different,
a pain he now knows he can heal,
through love and through care, and the joy the two share,
as they rear their babies into a life so real.

The four spend their days on walks and through caves,
a forever bear hunt they do seek,
one unit together, through all kinds of weather,
their love paves the way,
as water grooves through a creek.

Their days are now happy, for they have each other,
a blessing they wondered if they'd count.

The voices are quiet, the noise is now low,
leading this life wholly devoted and slow.

A happy ever after, with swans for the proof,
lives ahead each morning they rise,
another day they can cherish, for they didn't perish,
but instead make the moments count most.

Their love for each other, and children, sister and brother,
is the prize of this life, that is sure.
No more reasons to seek, no more beliefs to unseat,
the brave boy willed into life a new cure.

How to Break a Woman

How to break a woman?
You can start off very small.
Ebb away her confidence, watch her stand a bit less tall.

Say the things that make her question who she really,
Erase her choice, and next her voice,
Make her panic from within.

Do the things that make her forget
The right she ought to have
The rights of every human being, hers now up for grabs.

Tell her that her pain's not real,
It's all up in her head.
Make her wish she'd never asked for help,
Keep her bottled up with dread.

Shock the spark clear out've her system,
watch her writhle, twist,
Make her wish she never was,
Now you get the gist.

Shred her from the inside out,
bankrupt her given worth,
Take away her joy and faith,
Shrink her place on earth.

Watch her body and herself lay crippled by the pain,
Hold her down with blame and frowns,
She's ruined by the shame.

Leave her there, cast her aside,
She's got nothing left to give,
She must be broken, out of tokens
to pay for her reprieve.

Walk away, the job's now done
Her rights have disappeared,
Do this again, to each woman,
roll us back oh so many years.

And while the eyes aren't closely watching,
She'll somehow still survive.
First shallow breaths, then next a step,
she's slowly coming to.

Everything of hers is gone, she cannot see herself,
The woman who she thought she was,
dissolved into something else.

But she's still breathing, heart still beating,
Her body's now a'changed.
"HOW TO SAVE THE NEXT WOMAN"
is now blaring through her brain.

Tender limbs pick up scattered pieces,
stand up a new game board
She can do this whole thing over,
past ceilings now her floors.

Watch her stitch herself together,
weaving to and fro,
A new template, an open gate,
to walk through on her own.

She has new tools, her eyes, her tongue,
her cracked wide open heart
She'll start small, she'll make some calls,
She'll plot out a fresh new chart.

As time bears on, she's gotten stronger,
her fuel's different in time.
The parts she thought had fed her soul,
no longer intertwined.

In the search for who she really is,
she starts to find herself.
The person who she wants to be,
for the world and for herself.

She's resourceful, she will find others like she is,
Those who were left, beat down, broken,
start to move their lips.

Soon they link up, now together, stronger than before
with wisdom wrought from piering pain
they'll no longer endure.
They use their voices, use their hearts, the parts that make
them whole,
To call for change, a storm to rain,
Equality for all!

So, how to break a woman?
In truth it can't be done.
For her to break, the earth would quake,
swallowing humanity whole.

It's time the world understands
what true strength truly means,
It can't be taken, only shaken,
because woman can still dream:

Of a world where women matter
as much as the dear men.
So grab a pen and fresh new lens,
Disrupt this old pattern.
Not us versus them, we're all humans,
We can end this deadly trend.

It's Time for New Tech!

Tech leaders, Tech leaders, they call the trends,
But Tech leaders, Tech leaders, are they foes or friends?
Tech leaders, Tech leaders, doth fill your cups,
Tech leaders, Tech leaders, oh please listen up.

Tech leaders, Tech leaders, why so wan?
Tech leaders, Tech leaders, you made this plan.
Where you would fund but *just* white men.

Tech leaders, Tech leaders, stand no more
On shoulders of the giants 'fore
Tech leaders, Tech leaders, it's your time to rise
You see, the tide has turned before your very eyes.

Tech leaders, Tech leaders, created vile,
spent the data from our smiles.
But Tech leaders also created good,
lifted people throughout the globe.

So Tech leaders, Tech leaders, what now to do?
Choose a different path or two?

To make good tech that helps us all,
All us with voices, big and small.

These new Tech leaders look like you,
ones with smarts and clear points of view.

Those with skills in math and science,
those who know how to engineer appliances.

Those who are skilled at seeing a vision,
those who are skilled at checking derision.

Those who are skilled at staying the course,
and those who are skilled at sensing the turf.

Those skilled in speaking from the heart,
those skilled in knowing how to get started.

Our future tech leaders need produce
goods and services that can more
than spruce-up outdated systems
and reject their funky, broke-down,
dead-beat rhythms.

Future Tech Leaders come from all around,
In the world is where they're found.
Hand-in-hand with people, side-by-side,
Hearts wide open, open, wide.

We need new leaders just like you,
it comes from within, this hope within you,
that you possess the skills for change
because you believe we're all playing the same game:

that we don't know for how long we're here,
so while it lasts, let's be clear:

Future Tech Leaders, this is our call!
We'll build new tech, solve real problems, big and small.
Let's use our powers, point them toward good,
and we'll watch our beautiful world evolve as it should.

SHOO-IN

It's called a ***shoo-in*** 'cause you're rigged to fit in
to the thing that they said that they want.

So when you find out that you missed the mark,
the pain also comes with deep shock.

You gave them the plan with all that you'd do
with the trust they can vest within you,

But instead they would choose the option that loses
the chance for you to keep going.

It's unclear ahead what will happen next,
though now you know that closed door,
wasn't for you, you'd never fit through,
with all your light that keeps you so ***big.***

So keep your chin up with your back
and your front and your eyes trained ahead to the light.

The next open door to a new room or a floor
will be up ahead in no time.

Surprise, Catastrophe!

A crash, a bang, an open flame,
SURPRISE, CATASTROPHE!

The shock that comes, a quick gut punch,
knocks you to your knees.

Shuts you down, you cannot think,
frozen, cannot move,
Act or attack, flee or just be,
too much happening to choose.

Inside your brain the vortex spirals,
twisting up the dials,
Controls are gone, there's something wrong,
and this will take a while.

You can't go back, it doesn't work
like that to turn back time,
So forge ahead, to find instead,
a new path to discover.

How to do it? It's always hard,
you wouldn't choose this work.
But trust you'll know just how to face
what's facing you to come.

So take a pause and hold your paws,
take stock of who you are,
your parts inside are to survive
what living has in store.

Soon it will be time to rouse up, ready,
to do what must come next,
it's in your hands, it's your command,
you're ready to expand.

So, how to start?
You need a team! An inside cavalry.
Know they're all ready, calm and steady,
your body's infantry.

First! Find Madam Take-A-Breath,
she slows to the pace of whales,
steady as the breath comes in,
deep inhales and exhales.

Feel yourself calm and cool,
you find the next right step,
In your breath, release distress,
you know just what to do.

Next, call up Lady 'Drenaline,
tell her to get LARGE,
to send the sparkles through your veins,
mount up to lead the charge.

Feel the tingle as it courses,
fast and through your blood,

now you can move, but take it slow,
sticky through the mud.

Last! Ring up Mrs. Fahrenheit,
'cause she can take the heat,
she absorbs the gamma rays,
victory fait accompli.

The heat's cranked up, her power's on,
irradiate the pain,
feel the fear pass through your body
as shifts unlock within your brain.

Hydraulics pumping, heartbeat drumming,
nervous system strong,
You'll see it happen, what comes next,
your own courage you will summon:

to make the choices you must make
to start to get on through,
the test you face to soon replace
the past that you once knew.

Feel yourself rise on up, your system's now aligned,
watch yourself move through with ease,
first now, then for the rest of time.

You broke the code, put down your load
and watch the earth still turn,
You shed those parts for a brand new start,
an ancient lesson learned.

It takes practice, but you will find
each time you face a feat,
when alarm bells ring with shock and stings,
you'll advance without retreat.

Healers & Seekers

Puncture pins with grimace and grins connect into my parts,
turning on the electric song of the universe in my heart.

Here I lay attached and synced up into and through the source,
where lives of old and stories told dance among the waves.

The peace is calm, the calm is peace,
it's still and sound and open,
healing up the scars and parts that long ago had broken.

In this space is where we find our parts who stayed behind,
they sacrificed with heart and soul so we could have this time.

So when you feel the hands on yours, holding holds you still,
you can know within the flow, it matters that you're here.

Take this with you, gentle soul, the healing in your bones,
for when you're out, so far out there,
you'll still find your way back home.

The pins are out, the lights come on, it's time to walk away,
but those who seek to heal and seek
come back often to this place.

36 is Double-Chai / The Lioness Inside

36, a second life, in Hebrew, double-chai.
This is the true story of a girl like you
who seized her beast inside.

The girl is now age 36, how did she find this stage?
A life ahead before her eyes, a hero sprung from her cage.

A cage in which she had to live to keep the beasts at bay,
best not disturb, best not perturb, please, mercy, keep away.

In her cage she could be safe, she could hide her key.
The key to life, no pain, no strife, if they'd just let her be.

She'd been born a kitty cat, asleep when she arrived,
She had needed not so much, just love to help her thrive.

But where she lived was not quite that,
a den of different sorts,
With whipping claws and viscous jaws,
among wolves who fought for sport.

Wolves who feasted on their own, made her a sacrificial lamb,
One who must live upon their terms, a life not worth a damn.

So of course they couldn't stop, wouldn't tie their hands;
couldn't keep themselves together, gave in to their commands.

They would take a pound of flesh
each time they rapped the bars.
Inside her head, she would retreat, wishing on a star.

And so at night, after the fright and fights had smoldered off,
they could rest, they had ingested love they'd starved from her.

With nothing left, she'd cry, bereft, no choice but shoulder on.

Weeping, wheezing, out of air, she'd drift away to sleep,
for a minute, in the dark, no longer theirs to keep.
She would doze, still in her clothes,
her own bedtime made up
drift off alone, there's no one home,
in this dream within her mind.

As she slept, in dead of night,
her star would shine its light,
when window panes and moonlit frames
would dance upon her walls.

Basked in the moonlight was a car, one driven by a beast.
A wolf in clothes all of its own, the sheep already eaten.

Every night while others slept, it crept up to her door.
She shrunk down, crouching, ossified, on the upper floor.

Now it stood on both hind legs, pawing the front door.
Its teeth were bared, its anger flared, a beast without a leash.

She was scared, worse, petrified, of what would happen next.
Was it sent, her messenger, or was it there to feast?

Or did it come to rip her from her cage of life
that kept her incomplete?

If she went, where would they go? She shuddered at the risk.
Awake in sweat, awake distressed, she never took the leap.

She would never learn its motives, she'd wake up just before.
Its car out there, red, roof bare, vrromming at her door.

This same loop played, on and on, for many, many years.
Because she hid the hate at home, she never faced her fear:
That who she was what they said,
the ones who bared their claws,
Those rules they made to keep her small,
flattened by their laws.

Even though she was now grown and fled the viper's nest,
She had to learn another world, new rules in every test.

And when she slept, though somewhere else,
her dreams same as before,
Now in new cities,
in new towns,
new mattresses,
new floors.

And in her dreams, she wasn't well,
though the waking noise had calmed.
Always whirring, always blurring, curtains always drawn.

She would still wake up afright, aghast at what she'd seen,
A ghost, or worse, perhaps a curse that passed as vivid dreams.

Then one day, she had enough,
the hurt had hemmed and hawed.
She looked down, shocked, she frowned,
her own blood dripping from her claws.

Next time she slept, the beast again she met,
she got a little closer,
What's the harm? It's been so long,
she really needed closure.

She watched closely, took it in, its shape revealed in time,
the animal she thought she saw was actually feline.

And now, what's more, it was a SHE, she gasped,
she screamed out loud,
All this time, through this whole rhyme,
she'd thought it was a HE.

She stood tall facing face to face, her gaze jagged and crazed,
Inside her eyes were craven lies: she'd created her own maze.

She'd left them, but their rot remained,
stamping out her spirit,
It festered there, though she was gone
she'd trained her soul to bear it.

A mirror to the center, to the bottom of the it,
She always had to get to where the pain would never quit.
Then it clicked, the lights came on, she knew her right away.
The beast was her, and they each other, a trick, a slight of hand.

Her mind had crafted its own play,
forever scripted,
hunted prey.

The beast was her, her broken spirit, split from all the screams.
But they were gone and they'd been wrong
Suddenly! New hope sprung from her dreams.

The dreams had been her purgatory, her cage within her story.
Proof of old wounds that remained, masking her true glory.

She would have to do the work
to heal her bruised and battered bones,
to face the trauma and the grief
that comes from broken homes.

When she saw life for what it is, a different way, her choice,
She reached inside and ripped them out,
she'd finally found her voice.

Then she felt it in her hand, the key she stashed away.
She had kept it all this time, waiting for this day.

This is what her key was for, it unlocked the pain and grief
that she'd worn inside her body, haunting in her sleep.

As she learned to reinterpret common ancient pain,
the key burst forth a golden coil, flooding through her brain.

She could now begin to see the chaos she had hid,
the pain from many years ago when she was just a kid.
She could see their rules were wrong,

that they had rigged the game,
they had tricked her into thinking she was the one to blame.

Without a name, a silent refrain, it twisted into shame.
Her mind had conjured up a beast,
a distraction from her pain.

She looked again to meet her beast,
she traced her hands with hers.
They were the same,
fierce,
untamed,
reframed
and ready for their reign.

They rose together, rejoined forever, a new being evolved.
Mystery solved, her maze dissolved, disintegrating to sand.

The gold inside began to weave a pattern,
strengthening her parts,
they'd been broken but could heal,
gilded scars streaked cross her heart.

She began to see the light, it shone from all-around,
her body now was beaming gold, her feet up to her crown.

She was calm, she was steady, she could see inside,
that she survived through all the lies
was now her source of pride.

She could rest, she'd passed the test,
she now would sleep in peace.

No more nightmares or cold, hard stares,
she'd brought them to their knees.

No more searching, no more hurting,
she finally broke free.

Leo born, Leo rising, Leo through and through.
No more cage and no more rage, she is a lioness.

Now at dusk, she rules with calm, she lives a different life,
Her body beams the key of gold
no more pain and no more strife.

Now she's here at 36, she's living double-chai.
Now she knows throughout her golden bones,
it's time for her to shine.

Now she lives her life, her own, one of her own design.
A lionheart, uncaged on hope, she lives her double-chai.

A husky spotted with
the engine running,
not unlike the animal
from the author's
childhood dreams.

A New Beginning

She left the pain in her neck up in Boston.
She's no longer living accosted.
Run down and depleted, though no more mistreatment
now that she sprints for her dreams with her partner.

They had to beg, deal, and barter
through the woods and the slaughter
for this time that they get every dawn,
when the sun up and rises as their lashes lift their eyelids:
it's happening again, what will they choose?

One day at a time, with rhythm and rhyme
heals their souls more and more every day,
four fresh starts ahead, cause they're alive! not yet dead.
please, mercy, go seize this day!

End on a High Note 🎵

Cheers to the fall, for you have the power
to make the hard call –
to make life more beautiful
than had it never happened at all.

Remember, my dear,
your choices the same:
choose joy or choose pain.

You can start to play by your rules.

EPILOGUE

Liberation

Chava and Morty are not yet forty,
but oh the lives they've lived.
They show up to wake you up
and free you from the chains.

The chains of life that break you down,
the ones that keep you small.
The ones that make you question
if you ever mattered much at all.

Their powers come from deep inside,
connected to the source,
The place of origins where we're born,
when we're first set upon our course.

He is a sage of strength and heart,
of care and love and soul,
A spiritual guide with a lifeguard inside
who heals to make you whole.

She, of course, is life itself, the first of her to live,
Her light, alive, shines through her eyes,
her gift to give and give.

Now they're here, upon your shore,
standing, watching, waiting,
For you to take the leaps ahead
you've been too scared of taking.

Fear no more, the time is now, it is and always is.
Take the prize, it's you and your time,
choose life, it's yours to live.

A Goodnight from Mama Chava

Hunny bunny baby bears,
Mama's in the den!
turning down the sights and lights
as we ready up for bed.

It's time we rest our homes and bones
while inside we heal and grow,
to use again when we wake up next,
roll outta bed, feet on the floor.

Here's what you can dream
about as we dial down this night,
that your joie de vivre has set you free,
so you can sleep in peace.

Your parts inside are what make you thrive,
your own je ne sais quoi,
it's who you are when you feel the
sparks and heartbeats in your heart.

So goodnight my sweets until the morn
when again we pray we rise,
When fresh sunbeams streak 'cross our skies
and we get another try.

Goodnight!
Mama loves her
BRAVE LITTLE BANDITS.